The Spear of Azzurra

A  THRILLER

By Megan Stine and H. William Stine
Illustrated by Martin Sauri

Adapted from the teleplay by William Overgard

Random House  New York

Library of Congress Cataloging-in-Publication Data: Stine, Megan. The spear of Azzurra. On t.p. the registered trademark symbol "TM" is superscript following "Thundercats" in the title. SUMMARY: Lion-O risks the safety of all of Third Earth when he uses the spear of Azzurra to rescue two fellow Thundercats from a cave of evil. [1. Fantasy. 2. Cats—Fiction] I. Stine, H. William. II. Sauri, Martin, ill. III. Overgard, William. Spear of Azzurra. Television program. IV. Title. PZ7.S86035Sp 1986 [Fic] 85-19571 ISBN: 0-394-87879-5

Manufactured in the United States of America 1 2 3 4 5 6 7 8 9 0

THUNDERCATS and THUNDERCATS characters are trademarks of Telepictures Corporation.

Contents

1. A Visit and a Favor   5

2. Azzurra's Spear   14

3. The Thunder-Cutter   20

4. The Four-Day Drop   28

5. Honor   40

6. Tricks   47

7. Secrets of the Cave   55

1

A Visit and a Favor

Just beyond a flat, dusty desert in a corner of Third Earth, a large, lush, green forest spreads out like a dark paint splatter. At the edge of this forest, animals of all kinds— small and large, furred and feathered, friendly and hostile—build their nests and hunt for food. These animals never run in fear when a stranger enters their domain. Instead, like guardians of the forest, they judge all newcomers by looking deep into their eyes.

One summer morning, when the sun was

just rising, Lion-O, Lord of the Thundercats, approached this thick mass of green. He smiled when he saw the trees. At last, after running all night, he was nearing the Treetop Kingdom. But to get there, he had to pass the animal guards. Would they let him through, or would they try to bar his way?

All the animals froze as Lion-O stopped to catch his breath among them. Some began to growl and bare their teeth when he drew the gleaming Sword of Omens, source of the Thundercats' power. But Lion-O did not raise the Sword. Instead, scraping the ground with its point, he drew a picture of a long bow with a notched arrow. The animals, surprised, fell silent.

A fat, green-feathered snake slithered close and lifted its head high off the ground to examine the picture. Then, after staring at Lion-O for a moment, the snake hissed a command. Instantly the animals moved back to clear a path so that Lion-O could enter. Lion-O returned his sword to its scabbard and sprinted into the woods.

When he came to a place where the trees grew so tall and close together that the sky was obscured, he stopped and looked up. "I must see Queen Willa!" he called. "It is a matter of life and death!"

Although no voice replied, Lion-O received an answer—a shower of arrows flying at him from the treetops.

"Identify yourself!" cried a woman's voice from high above.

Lion-O peered up into the trees and saw only branches and green leaves.

"I am Lion-O, Lord of the Thundercats," he called, raising his sword with its magical Eye of Thundera over his head.

Arrows had fallen from the treetops before. But now a dozen tall young women wearing clothes of green leather dropped down to the ground on long thick vines. These were the Warrior Women of the Treetop Kingdom, and each of them wore a long bow and carried arrows like the one Lion-O had drawn in the dirt.

Lion-O immediately recognized one of the

women. Nayda, the strongest and most intelligent of all the Warrior Women, ran up to embrace him.

"It has been too long since you've visited us," she said.

For a moment Lion-O returned her embrace with happy affection. But the moment passed quickly. He remembered his mission to the Treetop Kingdom, and his face and voice grew serious again.

"I haven't come for a visit," he told Nayda. "Wilykat and Wilykit are in trouble and only Queen Willa can help me."

"Let us go to her, then." Nayda wrapped one of the vines around her waist. Then, waiting only for Lion-O to do the same, she launched herself into the air.

Nayda and Lion-O flew, swinging from vine to vine. And as they swung higher, the treetops began to change. Hidden among the branches and leaves was a village of small thatched buildings on wooden platforms. The Treetop Kingdom was just as Lion-O remembered it.

At last they reached its center and the pointed rooftop he had been looking for. Unlike all the other buildings in the village, this one was *carved* into the trunk of a tall, fat tree. It was the Queen's Council, where Queen Willa of the Treetop Kingdom sat on a large wooden throne awaiting Lion-O's arrival.

Lion-O and Nayda leaped to the platform and bowed to the queen, who smiled as she bid them to rise. Taller than all the Warrior Women by a foot, Queen Willa wore a magnificent cape of woven feathers and a delicate circlet of golden leaves as a crown.

"You promised to come more often, Lion-O, but it is a year since your last visit," the tall queen reproached him. "And you wound us doubly by coming alone. Where are our friends, the other Thundercats?"

"They wait at the Cats' Lair, as concerned as I am, Your Majesty. I've come seeking your help," said Lion-O. "Wilykat and Wilykit have gotten themselves into trouble again."

"But that is what those two little ones do best," Queen Willa said with a smile.

"I know. But this time they have wandered into one of the Caves of Azzurra and it has swallowed them up like a hungry beast."

The smile faded quickly from the queen's face.

"Dear Lion-O," she said, "that cave is filled with unknown evil and terror. Everyone on Third Earth knows that."

Lion-O smiled ruefully. He was all too familiar with the legend of the evil magician Azzurra, who once walked Third Earth. It was said that when at last Azzurra was near death, he divided his evil forces in half and stored them in two caves. One cave was on the Plain of Fertility. The other was in this very forest.

Azzurra had worked his terrible magic on the caves in another way—he had created the illusion that they were normal. They looked dark, stony, and empty. An innocent passer-by, glancing at the entrance, could have no inkling of the dark forces that lurked beyond.

But one step inside would dispel the illusion forever. Anyone who ventured into the caves was instantly trapped there—for eternity.

Lion-O had told Wilykat and Wilykit more times than he could remember that the caves were forbidden. But unfortunately, as soon as the Wilykittens heard that something was forbidden, they couldn't wait to try it.

"We Warrior Women bear the responsibility for guarding the caves," Nayda said. "But there is nothing we can do to help anyone who is foolish enough to enter."

"Yes, there is," Lion-O said, much to Nayda's surprise. "You can give me the key to the cave."

"What do you know of a key?" Queen Willa asked Lion-O.

"I only know that one exists," said Lion-O. "Your Majesty, I must have it to save the Wilykittens."

The queen shook her head sadly. "You'd better go, Lion-O. I am afraid you know both too much and too little about the Caves of Azzurra."

"I cannot leave," Lion-O said firmly. "I must do everything in my power to help the Wilykittens. Anything less would be a betrayal of the Thundercats' code."

"Your angry face tells me that you think I refuse because my heart is cold," Queen Willa said, rising from her throne. "But I too have made a pledge—a pledge to protect Third Earth from Azzurra's evil powers! Follow me, Lion-O, and you will see for yourself why I *dare not* let you have the key."

2

Azzurra's Spear

Without another word, Queen Willa led Lion-O and Nayda away from the council and through the lush forest, until at last they came to a large rocky hill in a clearing. In the hill was a cave, and it was surrounded by Warrior Women on guard.

Carved in the rock around the cave's mouth were hideous creatures with strange weapons. There were other symbols, too, which meant nothing to Lion-O—except that they were exactly like the ones on the cave that Wilykat and Wilykit had entered.

Lion-O knew immediately that this was the second Cave of Azzurra. But there was a difference between this cave and the other one. An enormous wooden spear was planted in the ground right in the center of this cave's entrance.

"Imagine the most terrible pain, the cruelest suffering, the worst death—that is what Azzurra put in this cave," said Queen Willa.

As if to emphasize her words, the Eye of Thundera on the hilt of Lion-O's sword opened and began to growl. This was a warning to Lion-O that danger was near.

"What keeps the evil forces inside the cave?" Lion-O asked.

"This spear," said Queen Willa. She wrapped her fingers around the spear and there was a low rumble—half thunder and half moan—from inside the cave. "This is Azzurra's own spear," the queen continued. "After his death many generations ago, it was discovered that his spear could undo his magic. Ever since then, we have used Azzurra's spear to seal this cave. It is also the key which will open the other cave."

"Are you saying that if I take this spear to save Wilykat and Wilykit from the other cave, Azzurra's evil forces will be released from this one?" Lion-O asked.

"Yes. If the spear is removed for more than twelve hours this cave will open," said the queen. "My heart yearns to help you, Lion-O, but I cannot ignore the danger to Third Earth. Can you?"

Lion-O turned away from the queen, his mind racing. One cave had Azzurra's evil powers trapped inside; the other held Wilykat and Kit. Lion-O knew that Queen Willa felt the lives of two Thundercats were not worth the happiness of everyone on Third Earth. But there had to be another solution.

"How do you know this will happen?" Lion-O asked.

"There was once a spear like this at the entrance of the other cave. But someone removed it, causing Third Earth many centuries of suffering." Queen Willa was stern.

"Lion-O," she said, "that cannot happen again."

Without knowing what he was going to do next, Lion-O rushed to the mouth of the cave and pulled the spear from the ground. It burned his hands but he held on to it. Black smoke belched from the cave, and the

Warrior Women, too, acted on their instincts. They raised their bows and arrows and aimed them at Lion-O.

"Queen Willa!" cried Lion-O. "I cannot let Wilykat and Wilykit die. I will return this spear to you within eight hours."

"It cannot be done," said the queen. "The journey to the Plain of Fertility and back is too far. Do not let your heart make a promise your legs cannot keep."

"But I must do it. And I give you my word that it will be done. No harm will come to Third Earth."

Queen Willa listened to Lion-O's words and heard his pledge, knowing that he would not give it lightly. Her experience as a ruler had taught her to believe only what her eyes saw and what her reason dictated. But she had not forgotten what miracles courage and determination could work. She ordered her Warrior Women to lower their bows.

"To open the other cave, the spear must float in the cave's mouth with the blade pointing inside," she told Lion-O.

"How do I do that?"

"I have never had to use the spear," said the queen. "I only know the legends passed down from Warrior Women before me." Her green eyes flashed. "Take it and return to us soon."

"Thank you, Queen Willa," Lion-O said. "I will keep my word to you."

"Lion-O, you have not given your word only to me," said the queen. "You have made a sacred promise to all of Third Earth."

3

The Thunder-Cutter

As Lion-O ran through the Forest of the Treetop Kingdom, he sensed hundreds of invisible eyes on him. But he felt safe. He knew they were the keen eyes of the Warrior Women, watching over him until he passed safely out of their territory.

Lion-O could not know that four of the eyes watching him were anything but friendly. These unseen eyes, fixed unwaveringly on the Sword of Omens at Lion-O's side, wished only for his undoing. Even if he had looked, Lion-O could not have seen them, for they were watching him from a great distance.

Many miles away an ancient pyramid stood, flanked by four tall obelisks. This structure was a living monument to evil desires and cruel deeds. Inside it were Mumm-Ra, the ever-living mummy, and his ally, S-S-Slithe, the hideous leader of the Mutants. Together they watched Lion-O by peering into the smoking stench of Mumm-Ra's simmering cauldron.

"If we can prevent Lion-O from returning that spear on time, just think of our rewards!" Mumm-Ra said with twisted glee. "We will prove him to be a liar to Queen Willa. We will discredit all of the Thundercats forever. And we will release the evils from Azzurra's cave in the Treetop Kingdom onto Third Earth. Not bad for an afternoon's work!"

"But how can we prevent him?" S-S-Slithe asked. He walked to and from the cauldron, which provided the only light inside the gloom of the pyramid. "I know! Maybe young Lion-O will s-s-slip and break his leg. Then he will never reach the cave."

Mumm-Ra stood back from the cauldron and looked at the Mutant through glowing eyes. "S-S-Slithe, you spend so much time thinking with so few results," he snarled.

"Hard words from someone who's half eaten away by worms and time," answered S-S-Slithe, smiling to mask his true feelings.

Mumm-Ra shuddered. For an instant he considered shoving the foolish Mutant into the cauldron. But he had better plans for the bubbling pot.

"S-S-Slithe, if we wish misfortune to befall the young Thundercat, we cannot just wait for something to happen to him," Mumm-Ra said with contempt. "We must *make* something happen to him!"

"But, Mumm-Ra, the Sword of Omens. What can we do against it?" S-S-Slithe asked almost pleadingly. "Every day it seems to grow in power."

"Sword!" shouted Mumm-Ra suddenly, as though S-S-Slithe had insulted him. "I'll show you a sword!"

Mumm-Ra spread his arms wide and stretched his fingers toward the ceiling of the pyramid. Angry sparks—white and red—crackled between his fingers as if trying to break free. Then Mumm-Ra pointed his hands in front of him and bolts of lightning flew from his fingers.

"Here's a *sword*!" he shouted, laughing cruelly.

The lightning bolts came together in a flash, and there, floating in midair, was a powerful arm. In its hand was a six-foot-long sword with a shiny, sharp, curved blade. As S-S-Slithe watched with his mouth agape, the arm began to swing the sword, slicing the air with long, quick strokes.

Mumm-Ra laughed again and again and hurled lightning from his fingertips. With every bolt, more of the body appeared—first a head, then another arm, then a torso, legs, and feet.

The sword wielder became a great Japanese warrior, whose black hair was pulled back in a topknot, and whose sharp, dark eyes glared ferociously at Mumm-Ra and S-S-Slithe.

"What is this place?" he asked, speaking as much to himself as to the two evil allies.

Mumm-Ra stepped forward, keeping his eyes on the gleaming sword.

"I, Mumm-Ra, ever-living shogun of Third Earth, have brought you here to my service. I will reward you with an empire of your own!"

The warrior's arms moved too fast to be seen. One second the sword was poised in midair. The next instant it sliced the ground in front of Mumm-Ra's feet.

Even though S-S-Slithe was standing quite far away, he jumped back in fear.

"My sword and skills cannot be bought, Mumm-Ra-san," said the warrior. "I am a samurai. I fight only for honor."

"And that is exactly why you are here," Mumm-Ra said, motioning the samurai toward the still-bubbling cauldron with a sweep of his hand.

When the steam from the cauldron parted, images of the Thundercats in combat with the Mutants could be seen in the depths of the dark, churning liquid. There was Panthro executing his karate moves, Tygra cracking his bola whip, Cheetara running at blurring speed, and Wilykit and Wilykat mischievously tripping up one dull-witted Mutant after another.

"My empire is threatened by evil invaders," Mumm-Ra told the samurai. "See how they attack my peace-loving servants?"

S-S-Slithe, in the corner, coughed loudly to keep himself from laughing at Mumm-Ra's bald lies.

The steam swirled over the mouth of the pot and then cleared. This time a picture of Lion-O, brandishing the gleaming Sword of Omens, was revealed in the depths.

"The villains are led by this powerful warrior," Mumm-Ra said.

The samurai snarled. "He is a boy."

"His skill with a sword is unmatched," Mumm-Ra said slyly.

In anger, the samurai raised his sword above his head and brought it down. The sharp steel sliced through Mumm-Ra's metal cauldron, spilling the wretched liquid over the floor and filling the room with thick smoke.

"There is only one whose skill with a sword is unmatched! It is I—Hachiman, who stands before you!" The smoke cleared and the warrior stood with his sword high in the air. "What is this evil invader called?"

"He is called Lion-O, Lord of the Thundercats."

Hachiman laughed. "Then it is truly fate that has brought me here," he said.

Fate and my magic, thought Mumm-Ra.

Hachiman waved his enormous sword once again. "They call this great sword Kaen-Kaeri—the Thunder-Cutter! Now I will go and find the Lord of the Thundercats! And when my Thunder-Cutter is through with him, he will think he was struck by thunder *and* lightning!"

4

The Four-Day Drop

When Lion-O finally reached the other Cave of Azzurra, holding Azzurra's own spear, he felt a chill slide down his back like cold rain on a hot, steamy day. *I am feeling the cursed magic of Azzurra's spear and nothing more,* he told himself—although his instincts knew better. So did the Eye of Thundera in the hilt of Lion-O's sword. It snapped open and growled its warning of danger. But if danger was near, it would have to wait, Lion-O decided. He stared into the deceptively empty looking cave and closed his mind to everything except saving Wilykat and Wilykit.

It would not be easy. It had already taken him longer to reach the cave than he expected. And now, try as he might, he could not open the cave with Azzurra's spear.

For the hundredth time Lion-O went over Queen Willa's words. She had said that to open the cave, Azzurra's spear must hang suspended in air in the mouth of the cave. But how? Lion-O wondered. How could that be done? He tried holding the spear up one way and then another. He used his left hand. He used his right. He even tried standing on his hands and lifting the spear with his feet. But every time he let go, the spear fell to the ground.

In frustration, Lion-O walked away from the cave and surveyed it from a short distance. There wasn't time for failure. Could he find another entrance? A new approach?

He glanced up at the summer sun. No longer overhead, it was beating him in this race. If he didn't find a way to open the cave soon, the eight hours would be gone before he could return to the Treetop Kingdom.

"Lion-O, Lion-O," voices cried from the cave. "Go away. We are happy in here. Don't come in."

The voices sounded exactly like Wilykat and Wilykit. At first Lion-O was happy to hear them, but then he realized the voices were a trick to deceive and discourage him. Suddenly furious with Azzurra's evil tricks and impenetrable magic, Lion-O heaved the spear toward the cave with all his strength. To his amazement, the blade stuck in the mouth of the cave—in midair!

In the next instant the Wilykittens came flying out and landed on the ground, eyes wide, faces pale. They blinked, saw they were safe, and leaped into Lion-O's arms.

"Lion-O, the cave was horrible," Wilykat said.

"We kept hearing voices saying that no one wanted to save us," Wilykit said. "How did you get us out of there?"

"By placing all of Third Earth in great danger," Lion-O said, pulling the spear from

the opening. He looked at the spear unhappily. "Now I fear that someone else may wander into the cave," he said.

"It won't be us! Never again, and that's my final word," said Wilykat.

"It's not *my* final word on the subject," Lion-O said sternly. "I'll see you two back at the Cats' Lair. And no games along the way!"

Lion-O stood there and watched them run—but only for a moment. Soon he too started running.

He ran across strange fields and over rocky hills, his legs aching. After several precious hours had passed, he came to a small lake, where he stopped and drank quickly.

"Sounds like you're out of breath. Been running hard, youngster?" called a voice from nearby. In his rush Lion-O had not noticed the small, ancient, furry creature drinking from the lake a few yards away. "Where are you running to?" the creature asked.

"The Treetop Kingdom," answered Lion-O, stretching his legs. "How far is it from here?"

"Six hours if you stick to the paths."

"I don't have six hours!" Lion-O cried. "There's got to be a shorter way!"

"There is," answered Lion-O's strange companion. "But it involves danger."

Lion-O didn't care about the danger *he* might face. He thought only of the danger to Third Earth if he arrived too late with Azzurra's spear. Only a few hours remained before the other cave would open and spew out its evil forces.

"Show me, friend. Please," he asked.

Without stopping his slow slurping of the cool water, the creature pointed a finger behind him.

"Thank you," said Lion-O before setting off again. "One thing more—what is the danger?"

"It's a hole in the ground, youngster, that's all—but it's not like any you've seen before. It's wide—so wide that you can't jump over it. And it's long—it stretches the whole way across the valley between two mountains of jagged rock, so you can't go around it. When you get to it, you'll probably just fall in. Keersplunk! You know what it's called, don't you, youngster?"

Lion-O waited impatiently for the strange old creature to finish.

"It's called the Four-Day Drop."

The young Thundercat froze. He had heard of the Four-Day Drop—and the stories were terrifying. The creature saw the fear on Lion-O's face and went on talking.

"They say the pit's so deep that when you fall in, you don't hit bottom for four days— hahahaha!"

The sky was changing hue, darkening as if for a storm. But a darker gloom was threatening Third Earth, thought Lion-O. He knew he couldn't delay any longer. With a word of farewell, he got up and ran in the direction of the Four-Day Drop.

Down a hill he ran, through a field dotted with brilliant flowers, then into a forest that was cool, shady, silent, and dense with tall trees.

The minutes ticked by and Lion-O measured them with the rhythm of his running feet. He was wondering when he would face the danger of this shortcut when suddenly he stopped—for there it was.

Lion-O approached the edge of the Four-Day Drop and the wind tugged at him, as if to pull him in. The drop was as wide and as deep as the creature at the lake had said. But he had left out one detail. There *was* a way across it!

A tall, slender tree, perhaps felled by lightning, had fallen across the mouth of the pit. Its trunk rested where Lion-O stood; its tip lay on the other side.

There was no way to know if the tree would hold Lion-O's weight. But his options were running out as quickly as his time. He stepped up onto the trunk, using Azzurra's spear for balance. The wind tugged at him once again. Lion-O did not look at the log, nor did he look past the log into the pit below. In fact, his concentration was so great that as he neared the middle of the log, he looked at nothing at all.

Then the log shook. Lion-O blinked in surprise. There at the other end of the log stood a short man with a black topknot, wearing a kind of jacket and trousers that Lion-O had never seen before. It was Hachiman, and he was testing the log by stamping on it.

"Hey!" Lion-O shouted, thinking the man hadn't seen him.

Much to his surprise, the man ignored
Lion-O's warning, jumped up on the log, and
started to cross over the pit. The Eye of
Thundera growled a warning.

"Pardon me, sir," Lion-O called. "But as I
started across first, I ask you, please, to back
off."

"A samurai never backs off!" snarled

Hachiman. So intent was he on crossing the log quickly that he failed to recognize something very important. Standing right before him was the very reason he wanted to get across the log: the Lord of the Thundercats.

"Does that mean that a samurai has no manners?"

"Is it good manners for a boy to stand in the way of a man?" said Hachiman. "I will teach you manners!"

The samurai drew his sword. And before Lion-O could say another word, Hachiman swung. But Lion-O was not Hachiman's target. Instead, Hachiman's sword came down on the log! The log shook from the blow but Lion-O regained his balance, thanks to Azzurra's spear.

"I will chop this log until *you* back off!" Hachiman said. "What do you think of that, impolite youth?"

"I think I must be facing a madman. Who else would risk killing himself and me just to avoid apologizing for a mistake?"

"Backing off is no disgrace for a boy!"

Hachiman shouted. He swung at the log again.

"Neither is admitting you're wrong, foolish warrior!" shouted Lion-O.

Hachiman's sword struck again and the log began to creak.

Because of his anger, Hachiman was blind to the fact that though arguments may last for years, slender logs cannot. At a final blow from the samurai's sword, the log split in two. And Lion-O, Hachiman, and Azzurra's spear plunged into the endless pit.

5

Honor

"Hai-i-i-i!"

Lion-O heard Hachiman's cry but did not see where he fell. He was too busy falling himself—with heart-stopping speed down into the drop. But the young Thundercat's lightning-swift reflexes did not fail him. As the half-log he had been standing on fell, he leaped, catching hold of the opposite half-log—the one where his opponent had stood. It swung down in a terrifying arc, and Lion-O clung to it with all his strength. Then, in the split second before it crashed against the rocky inside wall of the drop, Lion-O leaped again, and again he was successful. Now, thanks to the Claw Shield, he had a hold on the wall about fifteen feet below ground level.

Lion-O breathed a sigh of relief. But it came too soon: the Claw Shield began to slip, and he knew he mustn't delay his perilous climb up the wall of the drop. As he made his way up, slowly and with agonizing care, he could not help but wonder about the man who had confronted him. Who was he? Why in the name of the great blue heavens would he start a fight on a log that hung over a bottomless pit? *My questions will never be answered,* thought Lion-O. *He's paid for his foolishness—he must be plummeting toward the bottom of the drop by now.*

But Lion-O's thoughts were interrupted by a series of angry grunts from below. He looked down. There, about twenty feet below him, was the samurai, climbing up the Four-Day Drop. Inching stone by stone, wedging his great sword into the rocks for leverage,

Hachiman attacked the wall as though it were a battlefield foe. Then he came to a place, just below Lion-O, where the rock was solid and smooth. There was no way for him to climb any higher.

Hachiman looked up and saw Lion-O dangling against the wall of the pit. The samurai smiled, not because he was relieved to see Lion-O alive, but because he thought a solution was near at hand. "Reach down! Pull me up!" Hachiman shouted.

If he had asked instead of ordered, if in his voice there had been a single note of apology, Lion-O would have stretched out his hand to the samurai immediately. But Hachiman's attitude angered Lion-O.

"You're the one who got us into this," he said. "What were you fighting for?"

"For honor—the only thing a warrior fights for and dies for," said Hachiman. "Now pull me up! I have an important mission to carry out."

"Warrior, you are not the only one with an important mission," Lion-O said. He reached out and gripped the samurai's hand tightly.

"Pull hard. A tyrant awaits my sword. I must seek Lion-O as my master bids me."

The talons of the Claw Shield on Lion-O's left hand slipped and he slid lower into the pit.

"Why did you stop pulling me up?"

"Lion-O? Why do you seek Lion-O?"

"I am Hachiman, warrior to the wise and powerful shogun Mumm-Ra. He has commanded me to destroy the villain Lion-O and capture his sword," Hachiman said.

"Do you not know that *I* am Lion-O—the 'villain' you seek?"

Hachiman laughed. "So you will win our battle after all. That is as it should be. If *I* were above *you*, I would not save you. I would send you to your deserving death!"

"That is the difference between you and a Thundercat," said Lion-O as he pulled himself, and Hachiman, to the top of the pit.

Once they stood with solid ground beneath their feet, Lion-O said, "Warrior, can you now draw your sword against the man who saved your life? Will your honor permit that?"

Hachiman hesitated. He looked as though he were experiencing a kind of pain for which his training had not prepared him.

"No, I cannot draw my sword against you," he said at last. "My heart knows that would be an action without honor. Lion-O, you have been more than brave against one you knew was your enemy—you have been generous. But Mumm-Ra-san said that you oppose him. This is a strange planet."

"*Mumm-Ra* is the enemy of honor on this planet," Lion-O said. "That is the truth which he kept from you."

"I know it must be so," Hachiman said, reaching for Lion-O's hand. "A minute ago your grasp saved my life. Now let mine seal our friendship."

As the two shook hands, an animal in the distance howled, and Lion-O realized with a shock that night had fallen and the moon was coming up. His heart sank.

"Oh, no!" he cried. "I am too late!" Like a

wild creature, he dropped to the ground and
began searching frantically for the Spear of
Azzurra.

"What are you looking for?" Hachiman
asked.

"A wooden spear. I threw it down when
the log split. But it's gone!" Lion-O looked
everywhere until he realized the sad truth:

his aim had not been true. The spear, instead of landing on the ground, had fallen into the Four-Day Drop. Lion-O walked to the edge of the pit, his thoughts dark, his heart heavy. He would have traded his own precious sword for the Spear of Azzurra, if only it were possible.

Hachiman put his hand on Lion-O's shoulder and pulled him gently away from the Four-Day Drop.

"Without that spear, I have no pride, no honor, no hope for a peaceful life on Third Earth," Lion-O said. "I must go to Queen Willa and tell her I have failed to keep my promise."

"I do not know why your spear is so important," said Hachiman. "But perhaps this news will help. Today I saw your spear's twin brother."

"There *were* two of those spears!" cried Lion-O. "But the other was removed from its place years ago. Where did you see it?"

"In the pyramid of Mumm-Ra," answered Hachiman.

6

Tricks

As Hachiman and Lion-O neared the Black Pyramid of Mumm-Ra, they watched the moon rise even higher in the evening sky.

"I promised to return the spear to Queen Willa within eight hours. But that time has come and gone now," Lion-O said. He closed a heavy black cloak about him which he had borrowed from a traveler along the way. "My plan must succeed quickly or both Mumm-Ra and Azzurra will have their revenge on Third Earth."

"I still do not understand why we need a

plan when we have our swords," Hachiman said.

"Because Mumm-Ra will flee if he knows we have come to fight him. But if he thinks I have been lured into his trap, I might be able to lure him into mine," Lion-O said.

Hachiman nodded in agreement. Then he grabbed Lion-O by the back of the neck. The samurai half pulled, half pushed Lion-O into the foul depths of Mumm-Ra's tomb.

S-S-Slithe could not stop his eyes from widening at the sight of his greatest enemy, Lion-O, being dragged like a captured animal into the tomb. But Mumm-Ra assumed a pose of calm. He walked through the tomb, lighting a torch here with a snap of his fingers, conjuring a bubbling cauldron there with a muffled word.

"This is a pleasant surprise," Mumm-Ra said nonchalantly. "Hachiman, you have fetched this prize like a loyal retriever. You will be well rewarded for your work." Then Mumm-Ra put his hideous face near Lion-O's. "Boy, you do not fool me. I know that you have come for the Spear of Azzurra. Tell me, what have you done with yours?" Mumm-Ra's laugh seemed to blot out what little light penetrated the pyramid.

"This-s-s hasn't been your day, has-s-s it?" S-S-Slithe added with a sneer.

Lion-O had no time to be clever. Less than an hour remained until the evil spirits would be released from the cave.

"Mumm-Ra, I will make a bargain with you," Lion-O said.

"It had better be a good bargain," said Mumm-Ra, looking into his smoking cauldron. He motioned for Hachiman to bring Lion-O closer so he could see. There in the pot was the image of Azzurra's cave in the Treetop Kingdom. The Warrior Women gathered there were anxiously looking into the forest, then at the cave's entrance, and then into the forest again. It was clear they were waiting for Lion-O.

"Azzurra's cave cannot hold back its cursed forces much longer," said Mumm-Ra.

"Mumm-Ra," Lion-O said, pretending to

struggle in Hachiman's grip, "this is my bargain: Give me the Spear of Azzurra and in return . . . I will give you my sword."

Lion-O held his breath. Would his plan work?

"Hahahaha!" Mumm-Ra suddenly exploded, clapping his hands together. "I can barely believe my ears. Say it again, Lion-O! Say it on your knees so I can savor this moment!"

Lion-O pulled the cloak tighter around him and dropped slowly to his knees. As Mumm-Ra and S-S-Slithe came closer, he said, "Mumm-Ra, I will surrender my sword to you if you will give me the Spear of Azzurra." For once in his young life Lion-O was using his strength for an unfamiliar purpose—to mask his true feelings.

A streak of lightning shot out of Mumm-Ra's fingers, and the spear—an exact duplicate of the one Queen Willa had given Lion-O—flashed into Mumm-Ra's hands. He looked at it in silence for several moments.

"I am very proud of this spear," he said at last. "On that day, many years ago, when I had the courage to challenge Azzurra and steal his spear, I knew that nothing on this planet—or on any planet—would ever defeat

me!" Mumm-Ra's voice rang with icy satisfaction.

"And by removing that spear, you made Third Earth suffer for centuries," S-S-Slithe said admiringly.

"Yet all that misery and destruction meant nothing to me. What really mattered was that my hatred of Azzurra was finally satisfied," Mumm-Ra said, handing the spear to Lion-O, who was still on his knees. "Hachiman, stand him up so we can make a ceremony of this."

Hachiman obeyed quickly and pulled Lion-O to his feet.

"Now give me your sword, Lion-O," commanded Mumm-Ra.

Lion-O held Azzurra's spear in one hand. All eyes followed his other hand as he reached into his cloak. Lion-O could have run with the spear, but he too wanted the satisfaction of seeing his enemy defeated. He drew forth the sword that hung at his waist and handed it to Mumm-Ra.

"What is this?" Mumm-Ra shouted. He

dropped the bright curved sword angrily. As it fell to the ground with a deafening clang, he clenched his bony fists and shook them at Lion-O.

"That is the ancient sword of a samurai warrior!" cried Hachiman indignantly. "It is called the Thunder-Cutter!"

"Lion-O!" Mumm-Ra cried. "We bargained for the Sword of Omens. Give it to me. It is mine!"

"We bargained only for *my* sword, Mumm-Ra," Lion-O said with a smile. "It just so happens that Hachiman and I traded swords before we got here. But thanks for the spear."

"You'll never leave here with it!" S-S-Slithe shouted.

"Hand!" Lion-O called. Instantly the Sword of Omens leaped from Hachiman's side to Lion-O's hand. "Ho!" And the Sword obeyed Lion-O's second command, growing to its full length.

In their surprise and confusion, Mumm-Ra and S-S-Slithe had not noticed that Hachiman had also reclaimed his own sword.

It gleamed menacingly as he sliced the air with it.

"Hurry to the cave, Lion-O," Hachiman said. "The Thunder-Cutter and I will stay behind to entertain our friends. It seems they'd like a fight."

"Go, Lion-O," Mumm-Ra said with a sneer. "Take the spear to Azzurra's cave. It is too late for you to do anything now. I have seen to that."

"It is never too late," Lion-O called from the entrance of the pyramid. "Thunder-Thunder-Thunder-Thundercats—Ho!"

. Following the ancient command, the Thundercats' insignia shot out from the Eye of Thundera and into the sky. By the time Lion-O reached the Cave of Azzurra, he knew the other Thundercats would be waiting for him there.

Then Lion-O took off at top speed—which was considerably slower than the swift sprint he had used at the start of the day—with only one thought in his mind. Would he reach the Cave of Azzurra in time?

7

Secrets of the Cave

When he reached the dark green forest surrounding the Treetop Kingdom, Lion-O could run no farther. All of his muscles were numb beyond aching. Still, his senses were not entirely dead. He felt, as he walked among the trees, that something in the forest had changed.

If disaster had not yet poured from the Cave of Azzurra, the evil forces were at least seeping out, already playing chaotic games with the peace on Third Earth.

One of the guardian animals, hiding in the

55

tall grass, suddenly leaped out at Lion-O, snarling in anger. At first Lion-O raised Azzurra's spear to protect himself, but there was no need for that. They stared at each other silently. The animal's eyes asked, "How could you do this to us?" The Thundercat's eyes answered, "I had to try. I had to save the lives of my friends."

The animal lay down sadly and let Lion-O pass. Through the dense forest toward the cave itself, Lion-O dragged his tired legs. He still did not know whether he was too late to seal the cave.

Near the Treetop Kingdom, Lion-O stumbled on a sharp rock.

The ground felt cool on his cheek and, in his exhaustion, almost comforting. But what was that cracking sound? Lion-O stood up slowly, hoping with all his being that what he feared was not true. But it was. Azzurra's spear had hit the rock when Lion-O fell. The wood, so old and dry, had bent, then shattered and finally split under the weight of his fall!

Lion-O's heart broke in as many pieces. Had he solved the puzzle of the spear, faced the Four-Day Drop, fought to win Hachiman's friendship, and vanquished the cunning Mumm-Ra—all for nothing? Was Third Earth to be visited by Azzurra's evils simply because of a rock in the darkness? Had he released Wilykit and Wilykat from the cave only to make them suffer along with everyone else?

Lion-O felt sick, angry, desperate, and even afraid.

He walked on a little farther until he came to the cave. Warrior Women, their bows and arrows ready, flanked its entrance in a wide semicircle. Inside the semicircle, closer to the entrance, were the Thundercats. They too held their weapons ready.

From the mouth of the cave came a strange low rumble. *Like a monster awakening from a drowsy sleep,* thought Lion-O. The walls inside the cave, once dark, now glowed.

"Lion-O!" Wilykat and Wilykit called as he came near.

Nayda reached him first. Reaching out to support him, she said, "Lion-O, I knew you would come. But it is almost too late. Where is the spear?"

"I don't have the spear," Lion-O said. "I have failed."

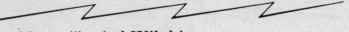

"Oh, no!" cried Wilykit.

No one else could find voice or words.

"I thought I could do it," said Lion-O. "But I misjudged the obstacles that would face me. I would have fought the fiercest monster. But my enemy wasn't a monster. It was just a rock. I didn't see it in the dark."

"You did what you had to do," Panthro said finally.

Lion-O found no comfort in Panthro's words. Instead, he pushed his way to the mouth of Azzurra's cave. When the horrors were released, he wanted to be the first to challenge them—even if it meant his death.

Tygra escorted Queen Willa over to Lion-O and they stood side by side at the mouth of the cave.

"When I told you that your promise was an impossible one to keep, Lion-O," the queen said, "I was not doubting you. But I knew the odds you faced."

"I see that now, Your Majesty," Lion-O said. "But if I had said my mission was impossible *before* I tried it, what would have happened to Wilykat and Wilykit?"

"I cannot even imagine," the queen replied. Her hand came to rest on his shoulder. "Do not fear, my young friend. We will be at your side—whatever happens."

Then a flash of brilliant orange light exploded deep within the cave. The ground began to shake, the air grew thin, and the rumbling in the cave grew louder still. It was as if something terrible was trying to break through the cave to freedom.

Lion-O, ready to battle Azzurra's evil powers, drew forth the Sword of Omens. There was shadowy movement inside the cave, and the earth-pounding noise grew deafening.

The sky exploded with thunder and lightning. Rain began to fall, blurring Lion-O's vision. For a moment he could see only dark shapes emerging from the cave. Then his vision cleared. Before his astonished eyes, droves of beautiful prancing animals and flocks of brightly colored birds, some walking, some flying, spilled out of the cave. Lion-O's breath stopped for a moment. Never in his life had he seen creatures such as these—wild, delicate, shimmering like a brilliant, unearthly rainbow.

Suddenly, as if it were a showery spring day and not a steamy summer night, the ground of Third Earth burst into blossom.

"What is happening?" cried Wilykat.

Queen Willa laughed, stroking the wings of a noisy orange bird. "There is only one explanation," she said. "Azzurra is returning all that he stole and hid from Third Earth. He kept his evil forces in one cave. But who could have known that in this one he locked away the goodness in him that he never wanted us to see?"

"Lion-O! Isn't it wonderful?" Nayda asked as the last of the animals ran from the cave. "If you had sealed the cave again, all of this joy would have been locked up forever."

Lion-O tried to smile as the warm rain washed across his face. But as the others danced and played and petted the animals, he could not forget how different things might have been. The cave might have held an unbearable parcel of horror and suffering, and he—Lord of the Thundercats—would have been responsible for its release! *In truth, all leaders are vulnerable to failure,* Lion-O thought to himself. *That is why we must make doubly sure of the goodness of our cause.*

Much later, returning to the Cats' Lair in

the ThunderTank, the Thundercats passed a short, powerful figure walking the road alone. At Lion-O's command, Panthro stopped the tank and Lion-O stepped out to tell Hachiman what had happened. He thanked the samurai for his help.

"I do not understand this planet," Hachiman said. "You failed on your mission. Yet you are wearing garlands of blossoms around your neck."

"In my celebration I have not forgotten— nor will I ever forget—the danger Third Earth faced because of me," Lion-O said.

"And you say that you live by a code of honor," Hachiman continued, "but was it honorable to get Azzurra's spear by tricking Mumm-Ra?"

"Perhaps not," Lion-O said. "But do not confuse the code with someone who follows it. The one may be perfect, but the other seldom is. We only do the best we can. Why don't you come and live among us, Hachiman? Then you will understand this planet and our code."

Hachiman did not reply. He simply plucked two flowers from the garlands around Lion-O's neck and smiled.

"Someday, my friend, I will return to you what I have borrowed," he said.

Then he walked away without turning back. He walked for days in silence, without sleeping, without eating, until at last he found what he thought was the loneliest corner of Third Earth.

But that was not the last Lion-O ever heard of Hachiman. Sometimes, when the Thundercats rushed to defend a remote, distant spot of Third Earth, they arrived too late to battle their enemies. Then, and only then, they would learn that Hachiman had been there already, defending right against wrong with his sword and his code of honor.

Each time this happened, Lion-O yearned to see Hachiman once more. But it was many long years before the two met again.

And that is another story. . . .